WHAT'S THAT NOISE?

Michelle Edwards and Phyllis Root

illustrated by Paul Meisel

CANDLEWICK PRESS
CAMBRIDGE, MASSACHUSETTS

"Sleep tight," said Mommy to Alex
and his little brother, Ben.

"Don't let the bedbugs bite," said Daddy.

"We won't," said Alex softly.

It was quiet in the hallway.
Quiet in the room. Quiet all around.

WHOOSH WHOOSH WHOOSH went the night noises.
WHOOSH WHOOSH WHOOSH

Ben sat up. "Alex," he whispered, "what's that noise?"

"Nothing," said Alex. "I'm tired. Go to sleep."

AROO AROO AROO

"Alex, I'm scared," said Ben.
"Will you sing me a song?"

"Just go to sleep," said Alex.

"*Please* will you sing me a song?" said Ben.

"Oh, all right," said Alex. "Just one song."

HOO HOO **HOO**

"Sing it in my bed," said Ben.

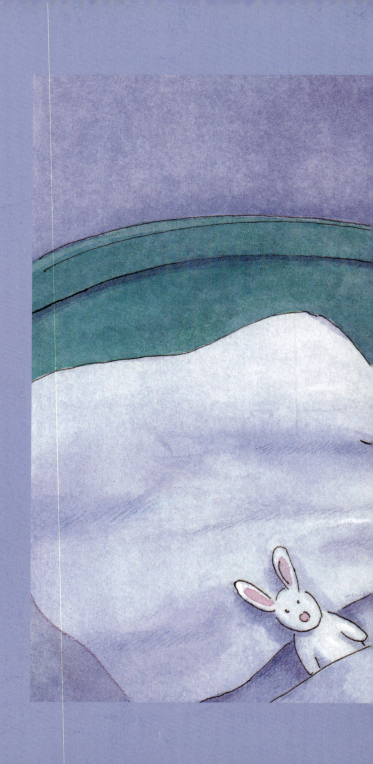

Alex looked across the room.

Ben's bed was far away across the cold, dark floor.

Alex didn't like to put his feet down on cold floors in dark rooms.

Something might grab his feet. Something might bite his toes.

A foot-grabbing, toe-biting something that went *WHOOSH AROO HOO.*

Alex hugged his bear tight.

"I'll sing it in my bed," said Alex. "Okay?"

But Ben didn't answer.

"Ben?" asked Alex.

Ben still didn't answer.

The room was very dark. Alex couldn't see Ben.

The room was very quiet. Alex couldn't hear Ben's noisy breathing.

Where was Ben?

Alex jumped out of bed.

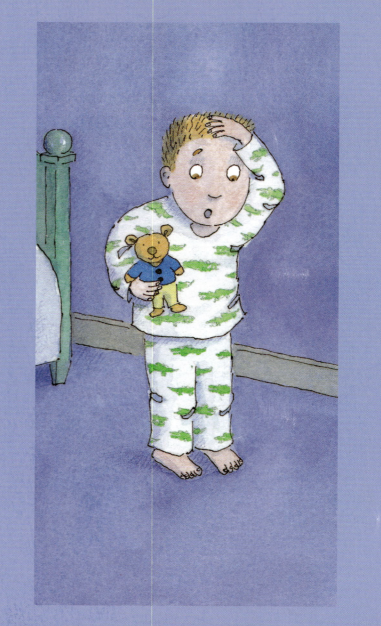

Thud went his feet on the cold floor.

Alex leaped across the room. His toes barely touched the floor.

Alex pulled Ben's covers back.

There was Ben!

Alex punched Ben's arm.

"You were here all along," said Alex.

"Yup," said Ben. "Now will you sing me a song?"

"Okay," said Alex. He got into Ben's bed, pulled the covers up around them both, and sang.

WHOOSH goes the wind.
AROO goes a dog.
HOO goes a baby owl.

HOO, HOO, HOO
sang Ben.

Alex and Ben sang until the
night noises all went away.

And it was quiet in the hallway.
Quiet in the room. Quiet all around.

With love to the memory of Emily Crofford,
a good writer and a good friend
M. E. and P. R.

For my sons — Peter, Alex, and Andrew
P. M.

Text copyright © 2002 by Michelle Edwards and Phyllis Root
Illustrations copyright © 2002 by Paul Meisel

First edition 2002

Library of Congress Cataloging-in-Publication Data

Edwards, Michelle.
What's that noise? / Michelle Edwards and Phyllis Root ; illustrated by Paul Meisel. —1st ed.
p.   cm.
Summary: Alex calms his younger brother when they hear strange noises at bedtime, but is he brave enough to cross the cold floor of their dark room when a foot-grabbing, toe-biting, noise-making "something" might get him?
ISBN 0-7636-1350-9
[1. Fear of the dark—Fiction. 2. Noise—Fiction. 3. Brothers—Fiction. 4. Night—Fiction.]
I. Root, Phyllis. II. Meisel, Paul, ill. III. Title.
PZ7.E262 A1 2002
[E]—dc21   00-065125

2 4 6 8 10 9 7 5 3 1

Printed in China

This book was typeset in ITC Highlander.
The illustrations were done in watercolor.

Candlewick Press
2067 Massachusetts Avenue
Cambridge, Massachusetts 02140

visit us at www.candlewick.com

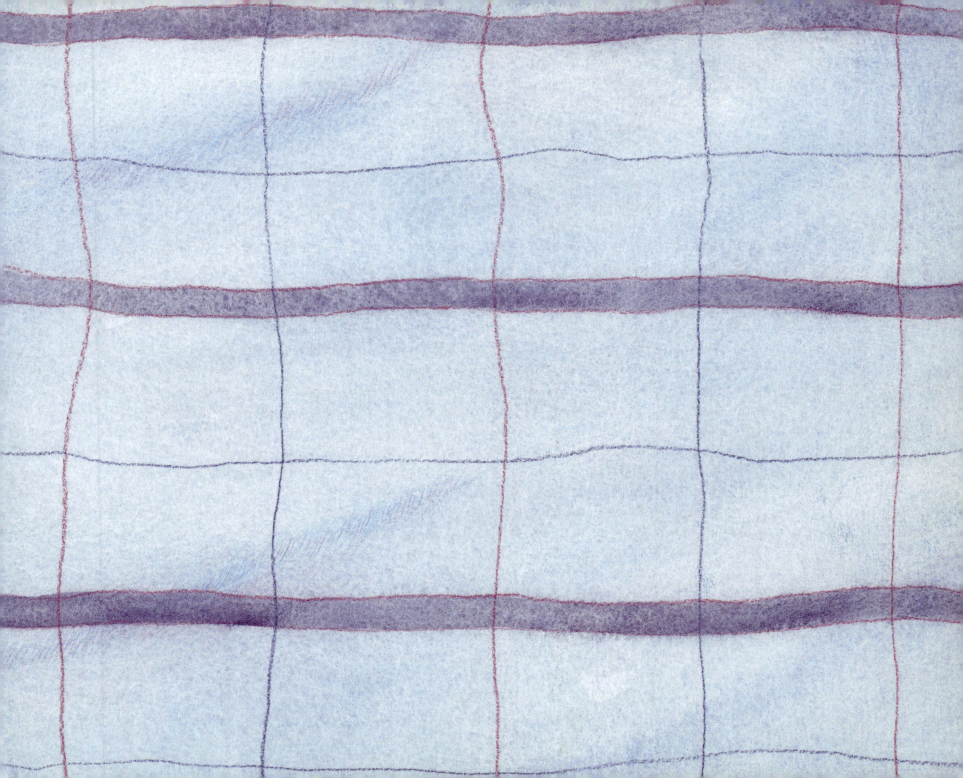

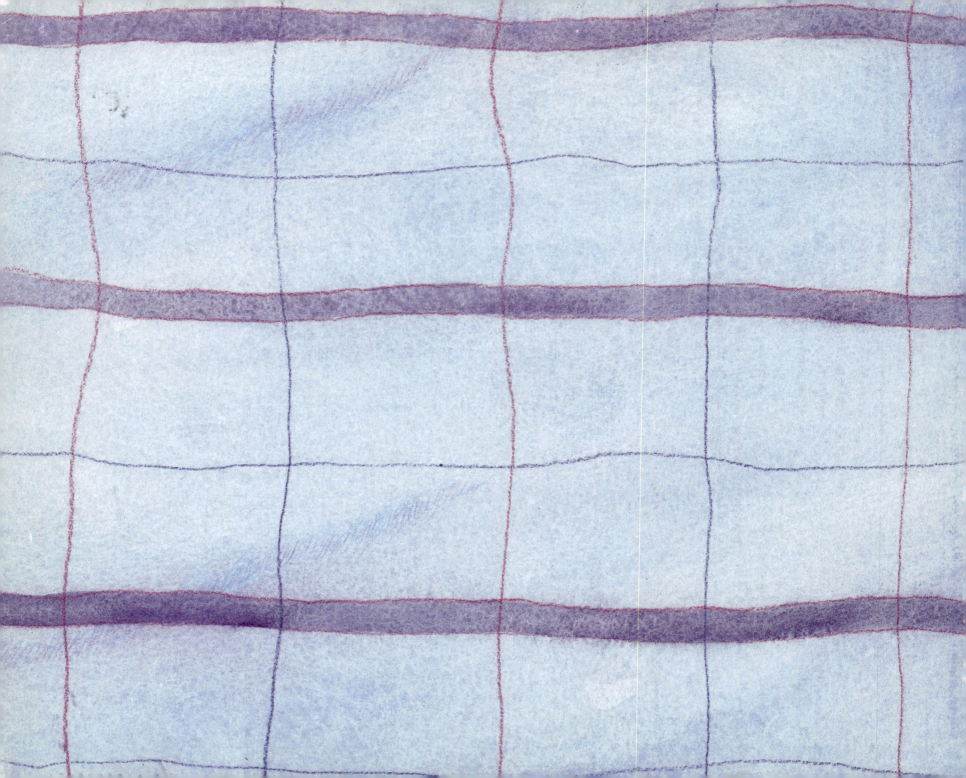